Wind in the Willows

Wind in the Willows

p

This is a Parragon Publishing Book
This edition published in 2000

Parragon Publishing
Queen Street House
4 Queen Street
Bath BA1 1 HE, UK

Produced by
The Templar Company plc
Cover design by small world

ISBN 0-75254-872-7
Printed in China

Contents

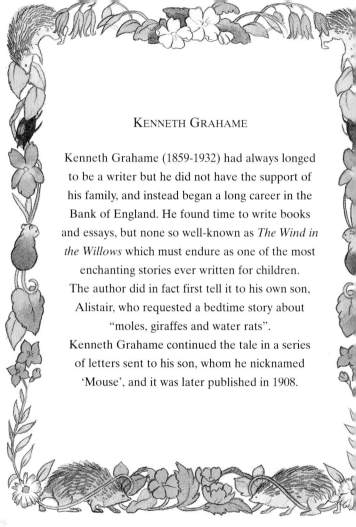

KENNETH GRAHAME

Kenneth Grahame (1859-1932) had always longed
to be a writer but he did not have the support of
his family, and instead began a long career in the
Bank of England. He found time to write books
and essays, but none so well-known as *The Wind in
the Willows* which must endure as one of the most
enchanting stories ever written for children.
The author did in fact first tell it to his own son,
Alistair, who requested a bedtime story about
"moles, giraffes and water rats".
Kenneth Grahame continued the tale in a series
of letters sent to his son, whom he nicknamed
'Mouse', and it was later published in 1908.

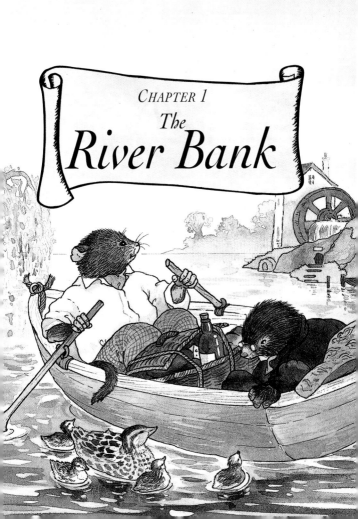

CHAPTER 1
The River Bank

The Mole had been working very hard all the morning, spring-cleaning his little home. First with brooms, then with dusters; then on ladders and steps and chairs, with a brush and a brimming pail; till he had dust in his throat, small splashes of white-wash all over his black fur, and an aching back and weary arms. Spring was moving in the air above and in the earth below, entering even his dark and lowly little house with its spirit of change.

It was small wonder, then,
that he suddenly flung down
his brush on the floor, said,
"Bother!" and "O blow!" and
also "Hang spring-cleaning!"
and bolted out of the house
without even waiting to put
on his coat.

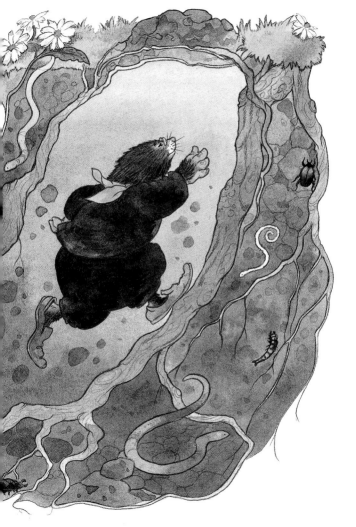

Something far off was calling him imperiously, and he made for the steep little tunnel which led to the fresh air far above. So he scraped and scratched and scrabbled and scrooged, and scrooged again. He scratched and scraped, working busily with his little paws and muttering to himself "Up we go! Up we go!" till at last, pop! his snout came out into the sunlight, and he found himself rolling in the warm grass of a great meadow.

"This is fine!" he said to himself. "This is better than whitewashing!" The sunshine struck hot on his fur, soft breezes caressed his heated brow, and after the long seclusion of his underground home, the singing of happy birds fell on his dulled hearing almost like a shout. Jumping off all his four legs at once, in the joy of living and the delight of spring without its cleaning, he pursued his way across the meadow till he reached the hedge on the further side.

"Hold up!" said an elderly rabbit at the gap. "Sixpence for the privilege of passing by the private road!" He was bowled over in an instant by the impatient and contemptuous Mole, who trotted along the side of the hedge chaffing the other rabbits as they peeped hurriedly from their holes to see what the row was about. "Onion-sauce! Onion-sauce!" he remarked jeeringly, and was gone before they could think of a thoroughly satisfactory reply.

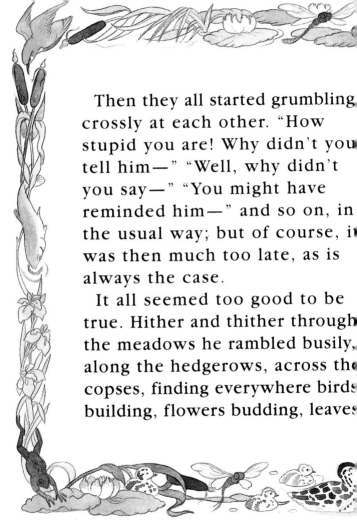

Then they all started grumbling crossly at each other. "How stupid you are! Why didn't you tell him—" "Well, why didn't you say—" "You might have reminded him—" and so on, in the usual way; but of course, it was then much too late, as is always the case.

It all seemed too good to be true. Hither and thither through the meadows he rambled busily, along the hedgerows, across the copses, finding everywhere birds building, flowers budding, leaves thrusting — everything happy, and progressive, and occupied. And instead of having an uneasy conscience pricking him and whispering "Whitewash!" he somehow could only feel how jolly it was to be the only idle dog among all these busy citizens. After all, the best part of a holiday is perhaps not so much to be resting yourself, as to see all the other fellows busy working.

And so, over hill and down dale, he meandered aimlessly along.

He thought his happiness was complete when he suddenly came to the edge of a full-fed river. Never in his life had he seen a river before — this sleek, sinuous-bodied animal, chasing and chuckling, gripping things with a gurgle and leaving them with a laugh, to fling itself on fresh play-mates that shook themselves free, and were caught and held again. All was a-shake and a-shiver — glints and gleams and sparkles, rustle and swirl, chatter and bubble.

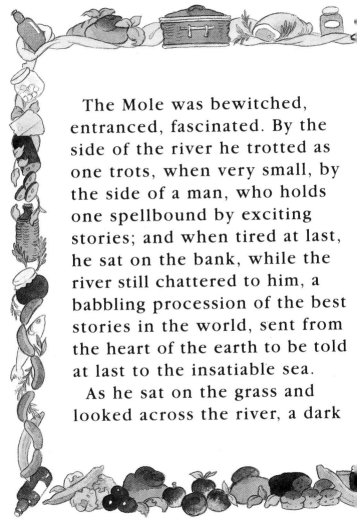

The Mole was bewitched, entranced, fascinated. By the side of the river he trotted as one trots, when very small, by the side of a man, who holds one spellbound by exciting stories; and when tired at last, he sat on the bank, while the river still chattered to him, a babbling procession of the best stories in the world, sent from the heart of the earth to be told at last to the insatiable sea.

As he sat on the grass and looked across the river, a dark

hole in the bank opposite, just above the water's edge, caught his eye, and dreamily he fell to considering what a nice snug dwelling-place it would make for an animal with few wants and fond of a bijou riverside residence, above floor-level and remote from noise and dust. As he gazed, something bright and small seemed to twinkle down in the heart of it, vanished, then twinkled once more like a tiny star — but it could hardly be a star in such an unlikely situation.

It was certainly too glittering and small for a glow-worm. Who or what could it be? Then, as he looked, it winked at him, and so declared itself to be an eye; and a small face began gradually to grow up round it, like a frame round a picture. A brown little face, with whiskers.

A grave round face, with the same twinkle in its eye that had first attracted his notice.

Small neat ears and thick silky hair.

It was the Water Rat! Then the two animals stood and regarded each other cautiously.

"Hullo, Mole!" said the Water Rat.

"Hullo, Rat!" said the Mole.

"Would you like to come over?" inquired the Rat presently.

"Oh, it's all very well to talk," said the Mole, rather pettishly, he being new to a river and riverside life and its ways.

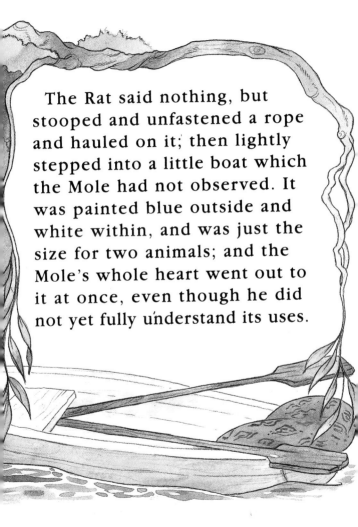

The Rat said nothing, but stooped and unfastened a rope and hauled on it; then lightly stepped into a little boat which the Mole had not observed. It was painted blue outside and white within, and was just the size for two animals; and the Mole's whole heart went out to it at once, even though he did not yet fully understand its uses.

The Rat sculled smartly across and made fast. Then he held up his fore-paw as the Mole stepped gingerly down. "Lean on that!" he said. "Now then, step lively!" and the Mole to his surprise and rapture found himself actually seated in the stern of a real boat.

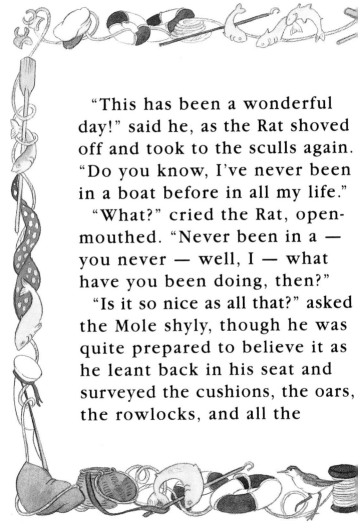

"This has been a wonderful day!" said he, as the Rat shoved off and took to the sculls again. "Do you know, I've never been in a boat before in all my life."

"What?" cried the Rat, open-mouthed. "Never been in a — you never — well, I — what have you been doing, then?"

"Is it so nice as all that?" asked the Mole shyly, though he was quite prepared to believe it as he leant back in his seat and surveyed the cushions, the oars, the rowlocks, and all the fascinating fittings, and felt the boat sway lightly under him.

"Nice? It's the only thing," said the Water Rat solemnly, as he leant forward for his stroke. "Believe me, my young friend, there is nothing — absolutely nothing — half so much worth doing as simply messing about in boats. Simply messing," he went on dreamily, "messing—about—in—boats; messing—"

"Look ahead, Rat," cried the Mole suddenly, for looming perilously close was the bank.

It was too late. The boat struck the bank full tilt and the Mole gripped the sides anxiously. The dreamer, the joyous oarsman, lay on his back at the bottom of the boat, his heels in the air.

"—about in boats — or with boats," the Rat went on composedly, picking himself up with a pleasant laugh. "In or out of 'em, it doesn't matter. Nothing seems really to matter, but that's the charm of it. Whether you get away, or whether you don't.

"Whether you arrive at your destination or whether you reach somewhere else, or whether you never get anywhere at all, you're always busy, and you never do anything in particular; and when you've done it there's always something else to do, and you can do it if you like, but you'd much better not. Look here! If you've really nothing else on hand this morning, supposing we drop down the river together, and have a long day of it?"

The Mole waggled his toes from sheer happiness, spread his chest with a sigh of full contentment, and leaned back blissfully into the soft cushions. "What a day I'm having!" he said. "Let us start at once!"

"Hold hard a minute, then!" said the Rat. He looped the painter through a ring in his landing-stage, climbed up into his hole above, and after a short interval reappeared staggering under a fat, wicker luncheon-basket.

"Shove that under your feet," he observed to the Mole, as he passed it down into the boat. Then he untied the painter and took the sculls again.

"What's inside it?" asked the Mole, wriggling with curiosity.

"There's cold chicken inside it," replied the Rat briefly, "coldtonguecoldhamcoldbeef pickledgherkinssaladfrenchrolls cresssandwhichespottedmeat gingerbeerlemonadesodawater—"

"O stop, stop," cried the Mole in ecstasies: "This is too much!"

"Do you really think so?" inquired the Rat seriously. "It's only what I always take on these little excursions; and the other animals are always telling me that I'm a mean beast and cut it very fine!"

The Mole never heard a word he was saying. Absorbed in the new life he was entering upon, intoxicated with the sparkle, the ripple, the scents and the sounds and the sunlight, he trailed a paw in the water and dreamed long waking dreams. The Water Rat, like the good little fellow he was, sculled steadily on and forbore to disturb him.

"I like your clothes awfully, old chap," he remarked after some half an hour or so had passed.

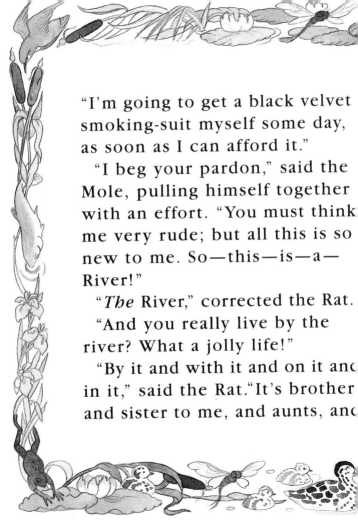

"I'm going to get a black velvet smoking-suit myself some day, as soon as I can afford it."

"I beg your pardon," said the Mole, pulling himself together with an effort. "You must think me very rude; but all this is so new to me. So—this—is—a—River!"

"*The* River," corrected the Rat.

"And you really live by the river? What a jolly life!"

"By it and with it and on it and in it," said the Rat. "It's brother and sister to me, and aunts, and company, and food and drink, and (naturally) washing. It's my world, and I don't want any other. What it hasn't got is not worth having, and what it doesn't know is not worth knowing. Lord! the times we've had together! Whether in winter or summer, spring or autumn, it's always got its fun and its excitements. When the February floods come, and my cellars and basement are brimming, and the brown water runs by my best bedroom window."

"Or again when it all drops
away and shows patches of mud
that smells like plum-cake, and
the rushes and weed clog the
channels, and I can potter about
dry-shod over most of the bed
of it and find fresh food to eat,
and things careless people
have dropped out of boats!"

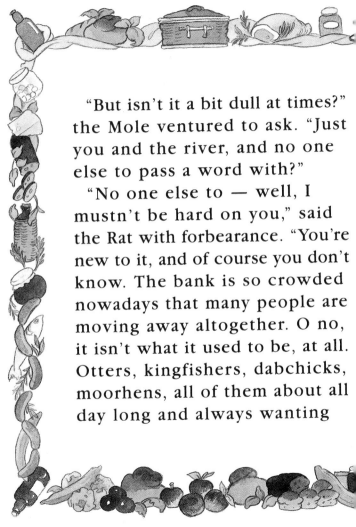

"But isn't it a bit dull at times?" the Mole ventured to ask. "Just you and the river, and no one else to pass a word with?"

"No one else to — well, I mustn't be hard on you," said the Rat with forbearance. "You're new to it, and of course you don't know. The bank is so crowded nowadays that many people are moving away altogether. O no, it isn't what it used to be, at all. Otters, kingfishers, dabchicks, moorhens, all of them about all day long and always wanting

you to do something — as if a
fellow had no business of his
own to attend to!"

"What lies over there?" asked
the Mole, waving a paw towards
a background of woodland that
darkly framed the water-meadows
on one side of the river.

"That? O, that's just the Wild
Wood," said the Rat shortly.
"We don't go there very much,
we river bankers."

"Aren't they — aren't they very
nice people in there?" said the
Mole a trifle nervously.

"W-e-ll," replied the Rat, "let me see. The squirrels are all right. And the rabbits — some of 'em, but rabbits are a mixed lot. And then there's Badger, of course. He lives right in the heart of it; wouldn't live anywhere else, either, if you paid him to do it. Dear old Badger! Nobody interferes with him. They'd better not," he added significantly.

"Why, who should interfere with him?" asked the Mole.

"Well, of course—there—are others," said the Rat slowly.

"Weasels—and stoats—and foxes—and so on. They're all right in a way—I'm very good friends with them—pass the time of day when we meet, and

all that—but they break out
sometimes, there's no denying
it, and then — well, you can't
really trust them, and that's
the fact."

The Mole knew well that it is quite against animal-etiquette to dwell on possible trouble ahead, or even to allude to it; so he dropped the subject.

"And beyond the Wild Wood again?" he asked: "Where it's all blue and dim, and one sees what may be hills or perhaps they mayn't, and something like the smoke of towns, or is it only clouddrift."

"Beyond the Wild Wood comes the Wide World," said the Rat. "And that's something else."

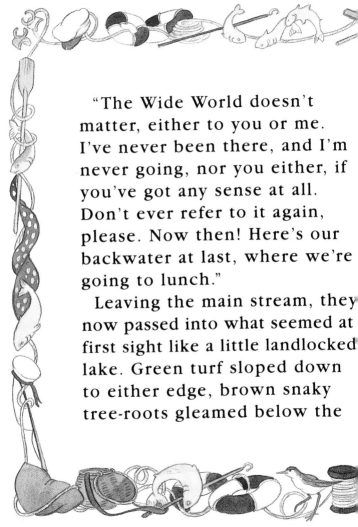

"The Wide World doesn't
matter, either to you or me.
I've never been there, and I'm
never going, nor you either, if
you've got any sense at all.
Don't ever refer to it again,
please. Now then! Here's our
backwater at last, where we're
going to lunch."

Leaving the main stream, they
now passed into what seemed at
first sight like a little landlocked
lake. Green turf sloped down
to either edge, brown snaky
tree-roots gleamed below the

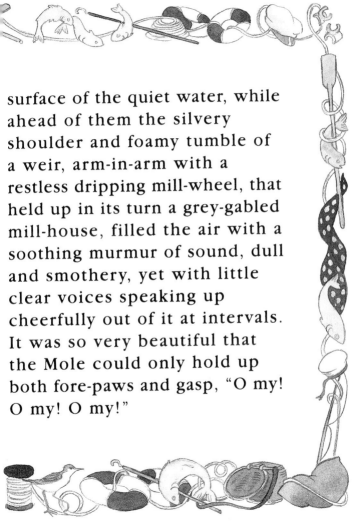

surface of the quiet water, while
ahead of them the silvery
shoulder and foamy tumble of
a weir, arm-in-arm with a
restless dripping mill-wheel, that
held up in its turn a grey-gabled
mill-house, filled the air with a
soothing murmur of sound, dull
and smothery, yet with little
clear voices speaking up
cheerfully out of it at intervals.
It was so very beautiful that
the Mole could only hold up
both fore-paws and gasp, "O my!
O my! O my!"

The Rat brought the boat alongside the bank, made her fast, helped the still awkward Mole safely ashore, and swung out the luncheon-basket. The Mole begged as a favour to be allowed to unpack it all by himself; and the Rat was very pleased to indulge him, and to sprawl at full length on the grass and rest, while his excited friend shook out the table-cloth and spread it on the ground, then carefully took out all the mysterious packets one by one.

Happily he arranged their contents in due order, still gasping, "O my! O my!" at each fresh revelation. When all was ready, the Rat said, "Now, pitch in, old fellow!" and the Mole was indeed very glad to obey, for he had started his spring-cleaning at a very early hour that morning, as people will do, and had not paused for bite or sup; and he had been through a very great deal since that distant time which now seemed so many days ago.

"What are you looking at?" said the Rat presently, when the edge of their hunger was somewhat dulled, and the Mole's eyes were able to wander off the tablecloth a little.

"I am looking," said the Mole, "at a streak of bubbles that I see travelling along the surface of the water. That is a thing that strikes me as funny."

"Bubbles? Oho!" said the Rat, and turning to the water, he chirruped cheerily in an inviting sort of way.

A broad glistening muzzle showed itself above the edge of the bank, and the Otter hauled himself out and shook the water from his coat.

"Greedy beggars!" he observed, making for the provender. "Why didn't you invite me, Ratty?"

"This was an impromptu affair," explained the Rat. "By the way — my friend, Mr Mole."

"Pleased to meet you."

"Proud, I'm sure," said the Otter, and the two animals were friends forthwith.

"Such a rumpus everywhere!" continued the Otter. "All the world seems out on the river to-day. I came up this backwater to try and get a moment's peace, and then stumbled upon you fellows! At least — I beg pardon — I don't exactly mean that, you know."

There was a rustle behind them, proceeding from a hedge wherein last year's leaves still clung thick, and a stripy head, with high shoulders behind it, peered forth on them.

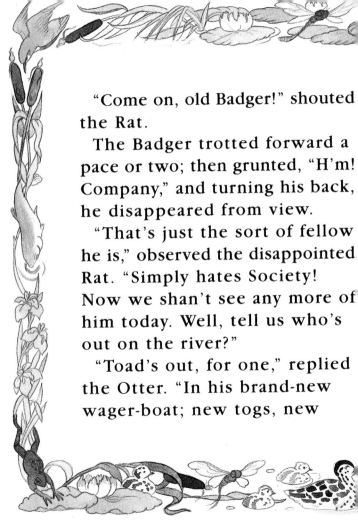

"Come on, old Badger!" shouted the Rat.

The Badger trotted forward a pace or two; then grunted, "H'm! Company," and turning his back, he disappeared from view.

"That's just the sort of fellow he is," observed the disappointed Rat. "Simply hates Society! Now we shan't see any more of him today. Well, tell us who's out on the river?"

"Toad's out, for one," replied the Otter. "In his brand-new wager-boat; new togs, new everything!" The two animals looked at each other and laughed.

"Once, it was nothing but sailing," said the Rat. "Then he tired of that and took to punting. Nothing would please him but to punt all day and every day, and a nice mess he made of it. Last year it was house-boating and we all had to go and stay with him in his houseboat, and pretend we liked it. He was going to spend the rest of his life in a house-boat.

"It's all the same; whatever he takes up, he gets tired of it, and starts on something fresh."

"Such a good fellow, too," remarked the Otter reflectively. "But no stability — especially in a boat!"

From where they sat they could get a glimpse of the main stream across the island that separated them; and just then a boat flashed into view, the rower — a short, stout figure — splashing badly and rolling a good deal, but working hard.

The Rat stood up and hailed him, but Toad — for it was he — shook his head and settled sternly to his work.

"He'll be out of the boat in a minute if he rolls like that," said the Rat, sitting down again.

"Of course he will," chuckled the Otter. "Did I ever tell you that good story about Toad and the lock-keeper? It happened this way. Toad…"

An errant May-fly swerved unsteadily athwart the current in the intoxicated fashion affected by young bloods of May-flies seeing like. A swirl of water and a "clop!" and the May-fly was visible no more.

Neither was the Otter. He had quite disappeared from view.

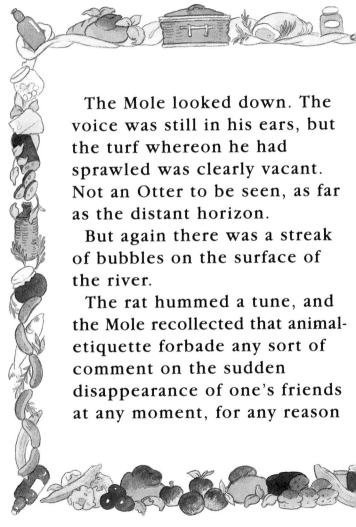

The Mole looked down. The voice was still in his ears, but the turf whereon he had sprawled was clearly vacant. Not an Otter to be seen, as far as the distant horizon.

But again there was a streak of bubbles on the surface of the river.

The rat hummed a tune, and the Mole recollected that animal-etiquette forbade any sort of comment on the sudden disappearance of one's friends at any moment, for any reason

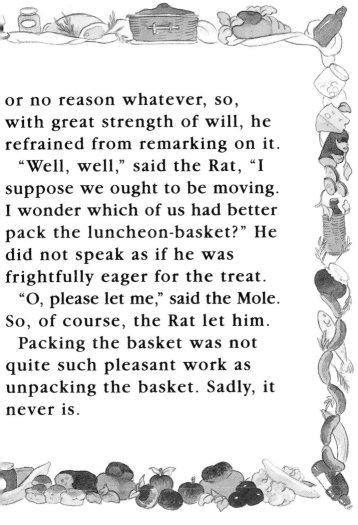

or no reason whatever, so, with great strength of will, he refrained from remarking on it.

"Well, well," said the Rat, "I suppose we ought to be moving. I wonder which of us had better pack the luncheon-basket?" He did not speak as if he was frightfully eager for the treat.

"O, please let me," said the Mole. So, of course, the Rat let him.

Packing the basket was not quite such pleasant work as unpacking the basket. Sadly, it never is.

But the Mole was bent on enjoying everything, and although just when he had got the basket packed and strapped up rightly he saw a plate staring up at him from the grass, and, when the job had been done again, the Rat pointed out a fork which anybody ought to have seen, and last of all, behold! the mustard-pot, which he had been sitting on without knowing it — still, somehow, the thing got finished at last, without much loss of temper.

The afternoon sun was getting low as the Rat sculled gently homewards in a dreamy mood, murmuring poetry-things over to himself, and not paying much attention to Mole. But the Mole was very full of lunch, and self-satisfaction, and pride, and already quite at home in a boat (so he thought) and was getting a bit restless besides; and presently he said, "Ratty! Please, I want to row, now!"

The Rat shook his head with a smile. "Not yet, my young friend," he said — "wait till you've had a few lessons. It's not so easy as it looks."

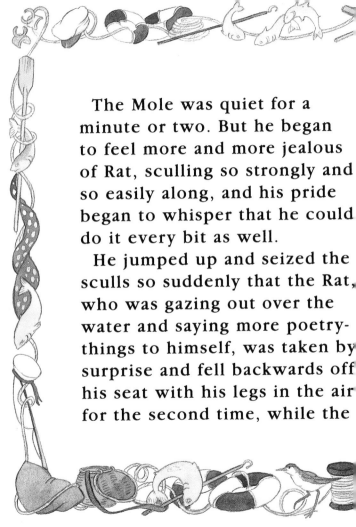

The Mole was quiet for a minute or two. But he began to feel more and more jealous of Rat, sculling so strongly and so easily along, and his pride began to whisper that he could do it every bit as well.

He jumped up and seized the sculls so suddenly that the Rat, who was gazing out over the water and saying more poetry-things to himself, was taken by surprise and fell backwards off his seat with his legs in the air for the second time, while the triumphant Mole took his place and grabbed the sculls with entire confidence.

"Stop it, you silly ass," cried the Rat, from the bottom of the boat. "You can't do it! You'll have us over."

The Mole refused to listen and flinging his sculls back with a flourish, he made a great dig at the water. He missed the surface altogether, his legs flew up above his head, and he found himself lying on the top of the prostrate Rat.

Greatly alarmed, the Mole made a grab at the side of the boat, and the next moment — Sploosh!

Over went the boat, and he found himself struggling in the river.

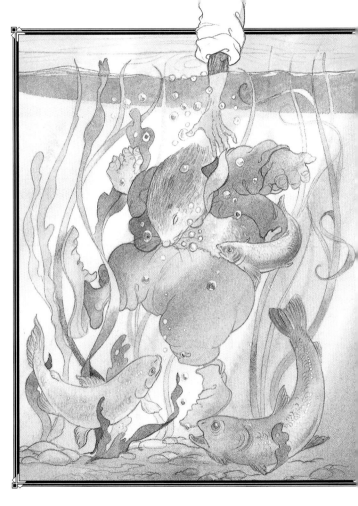

O my, how cold the water was, and O, how very wet it felt. How it sang in his ears as he went down, down, down! How bright and welcome the sun looked as he rose to the surface coughing and spluttering! How black was his despair when he felt himself sinking again! Then a firm paw gripped him by the back of his neck. It was the Rat, and he was evidently laughing — the Mole could feel him shaking, right down his arm and through to his strong paw.

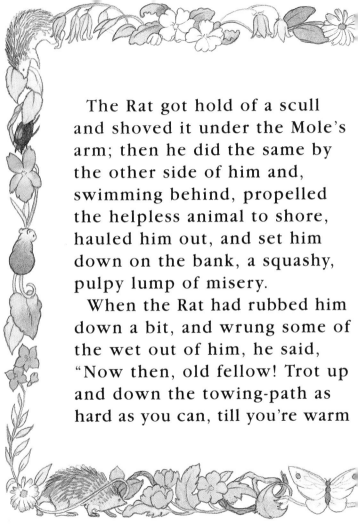

The Rat got hold of a scull and shoved it under the Mole's arm; then he did the same by the other side of him and, swimming behind, propelled the helpless animal to shore, hauled him out, and set him down on the bank, a squashy, pulpy lump of misery.

When the Rat had rubbed him down a bit, and wrung some of the wet out of him, he said, "Now then, old fellow! Trot up and down the towing-path as hard as you can, till you're warm and dry again, while I dive for the luncheon-basket."

So the dismal Mole, wet without and ashamed within, trotted about till he was fairly dry, while the Rat plunged into the water again, recovered the boat, righted her and made her fast, fetched his floating property to shore by degrees, including two plump cushions which were heading determinedly for the far bank, and finally dived successfully for the luncheon-basket and struggled to land it.

When all was ready for a start once more, the Mole, limp and dejected, took his seat in the stern of the boat; and as they set off, he said in a low voice, broken with emotion, "Ratty, my generous friend! I am very sorry for my foolish conduct.

"My heart quite fails me when
I think how I might have lost
that beautiful luncheon-basket.
Indeed, I have been a complete

ass, and I know it. Will you
overlook it this once and
forgive me, and let things go
on as before?"

"That's all right, bless you!" responded the Rat cheerily. "What's a little wet to a Water Rat? I'm more in the water than out of it most days. Don't you think any more about it; and, look here! I really think you had better come and stop with me for a little time. It's very plain and rough, you know — not like Toad's house at all — but you haven't seen that yet; still, I can make you comfortable. And I'll teach you to row, and to swim, and you'll soon be as handy on the water as any of us."

The Mole was so touched by his kind manner of speaking that he could find no voice to answer him; and he had to brush away a tear or two with the back of his paw. But the Rat kindly looked in another direction, and presently the Mole's spirits revived again, and he was even able to give some straight back-talk to a couple of moorhens who were sniggering to each other about his bedraggled appearance.

When they got home, the Rat made a bright fire in the parlour and fetched down a dressing-gown and slippers. Then he planted the Mole in an arm-chair in front of the blaze, and told him river stories till supper-time.

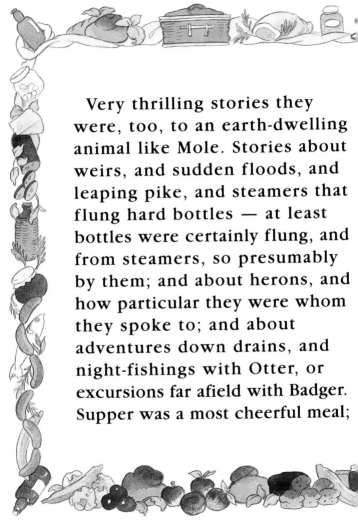

Very thrilling stories they were, too, to an earth-dwelling animal like Mole. Stories about weirs, and sudden floods, and leaping pike, and steamers that flung hard bottles — at least bottles were certainly flung, and from steamers, so presumably by them; and about herons, and how particular they were whom they spoke to; and about adventures down drains, and night-fishings with Otter, or excursions far afield with Badger. Supper was a most cheerful meal;

but very shortly afterwards a terribly sleepy Mole had to be escorted upstairs by his considerate host, to the best bedroom, where he soon laid his head on his pillow in great peace and contentment, knowing that his new-found friend the River was lapping the sill of his window.

This day was only the first of many similar ones for the emancipated Mole, each of them longer and fuller of interest as the ripening summer moved on.

He learnt to swim and to row, and entered into the joy of running water; and with his ear to the reedstems he caught, at intervals, something of what the wind went whispering so constantly among them.

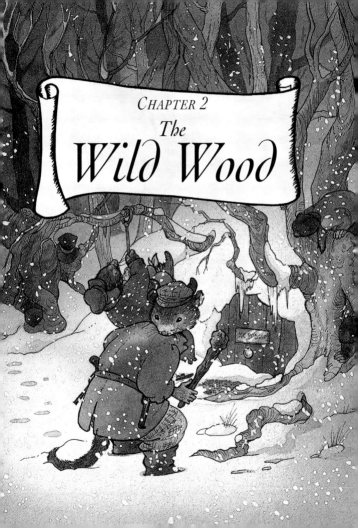

CHAPTER 2
The
Wild Wood

The Mole had long wanted to make the acquaintance of the Badger. He seemed, by all accounts, to be such an important personage. But whenever the Mole mentioned his wish to the Water Rat he always found himself put off.

"Couldn't you ask him here for dinner or something?" said the Mole.

"He wouldn't come," replied the Rat simply. "Badger hates Society, and invitations, and dinner, and all that sort of thing."

"Well, then, supposing we go and call on *him*?" suggested the Mole.

"Oh, I'm sure he wouldn't like that at *all*," said the Rat, quite alarmed. "He's so very shy, he'd be sure to be offended. Besides, we can't. It's quite out of the question because he lives in the very middle of the Wild Wood."

The Mole had to be content with this, and it wasn't until the summer was long over that he found his thoughts dwelling once again with much persistence on the solitary grey Badger.

In the winter time, in common with many other animals, the Rat slept a good deal, retiring early and rising late. During his short day he sometimes scribbled poetry or did other small jobs about the house, but the Mole had a good deal of spare time on his hands and so one afternoon, while the Rat dozed in his arm-chair, he decided to go out by himself and explore the Wild Wood, and perhaps strike up an acquaintance with Mr Badger.

It was a cold still afternoon with a hard steely sky overhead when he slipped out of the warm parlour into the open air. The country lay bare and entirely leafless around him, and copses, dells, quarries and all hidden places, which had been mysterious mines for exploration in leafy summer, now exposed their secrets and seemed to ask him to overlook their shabby poverty for a while. He liked the country undecorated, hard, and stripped of its finery.

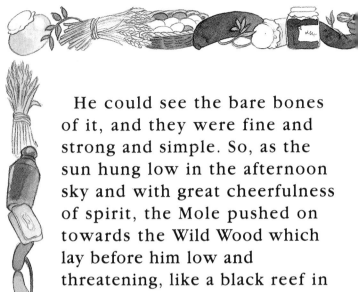

He could see the bare bones
of it, and they were fine and
strong and simple. So, as the
sun hung low in the afternoon
sky and with great cheerfulness
of spirit, the Mole pushed on
towards the Wild Wood which
lay before him low and
threatening, like a black reef in
some still southern sea.

There was nothing to alarm
him at first entry. Twigs crackled
under his feet, logs tripped him,
funguses on stumps resembled
caricatures, and startled him

for a moment by their likeness to something familiar and far away; but that was all fun, and exciting. It led him on, and so he penetrated to where the light was less, and trees crouched nearer and nearer, and holes made ugly mouths at him on either side.

Everything was very still now. The dusk advanced on him steadily, rapidly, gathering in behind and before; and the light seemed to be draining away like flood-water.

Then the faces began. It was over his shoulder, and indistinctly, that he first thought he saw a face; a little evil wedge-shaped face, looking out at him from a hole. When he turned and confronted it, the thing had vanished.

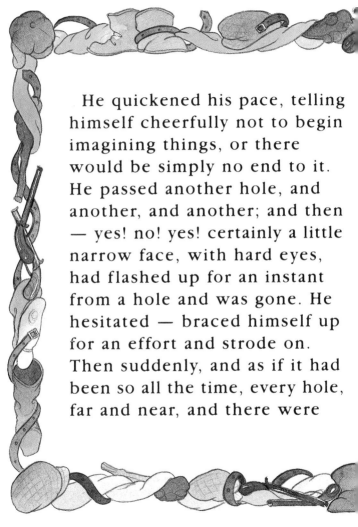

He quickened his pace, telling himself cheerfully not to begin imagining things, or there would be simply no end to it. He passed another hole, and another, and another; and then — yes! no! yes! certainly a little narrow face, with hard eyes, had flashed up for an instant from a hole and was gone. He hesitated — braced himself up for an effort and strode on. Then suddenly, and as if it had been so all the time, every hole, far and near, and there were hundreds of them, seemed to possess its face, coming and going rapidly, all fixing on him glances of malice and hatred: all hard-eyed and evil and sharp.

If he could only get away from the holes in the banks, he thought, there would be no more faces. He swung off the path and plunged into the untrodden places of the wood.

Then the whistling began. Very faint and shrill it was, and far behind him, when he first heard it; but somehow it made him hurry forward. Then, still very faint and shrill it sounded far ahead of him, and made him hesitate and want to go back. As he halted in indecision it broke out on either side, and seemed to be caught up and passed on throughout the whole length of the wood to its furthest limit. They were up and alert and ready, evidently, whoever they were. And he — he was alone, and unarmed, and far from any help; and the night was closing in.

Then the pattering began. He thought it was only falling leaves at first, so slight and delicate was the sound. Then as it grew it took a regular rhythm, and he knew it for nothing else but the pat-pat-pat of little feet still a very long way off. Was it in front or behind? It seemed to be first one, then the other, then both. As he stood still, a rabbit came running towards him through the trees and dashing past with staring eyes he cried, "Get out of this you fool, get out!"

With his face set hard, the rabbit swung round a stump and disappeared down a friendly burrow.

The pattering increased till it sounded like sudden hail on the dry-leaf carpet spread around the Mole. The whole wood seemed running now, running hard, hunting, chasing, closing in round something or — somebody? In panic, he began to run too, aimlessly, he knew not whither. He ran up against things, he fell over things and he darted under things until at last he took refuge in the dark deep hollow of an old beech tree, snuggled down into the dry leaves and hoped he was safe for the time being. And as he lay there trembling, he knew it at last, that dread thing which other little dwellers in field and hedgerow had met here, and known as their darkest moment — that thing which the Rat had vainly tried to shield him from — the Terror of the Wild Wood!

Meantime the Rat, warm and comfortable, dozed by his fireside. Then a coal slipped, the fire crackled and he woke with a start. He looked for the Mole — but the Mole was not there. The house seemed very quiet. The Rat called "Moly!" several times and, receiving no answer, got up and went out into the hall. The Mole's cap and galoshes were gone.

Outside the front door the Rat surveyed the muddy surface of the ground.

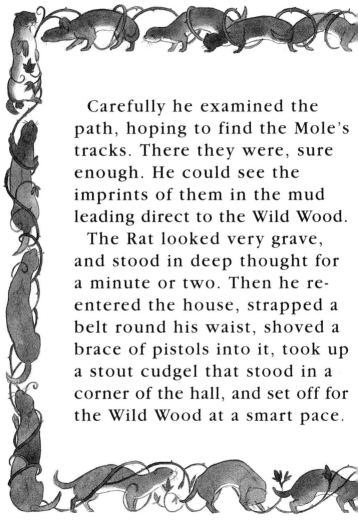

Carefully he examined the path, hoping to find the Mole's tracks. There they were, sure enough. He could see the imprints of them in the mud leading direct to the Wild Wood.

The Rat looked very grave, and stood in deep thought for a minute or two. Then he re-entered the house, strapped a belt round his waist, shoved a brace of pistols into it, took up a stout cudgel that stood in a corner of the hall, and set off for the Wild Wood at a smart pace.

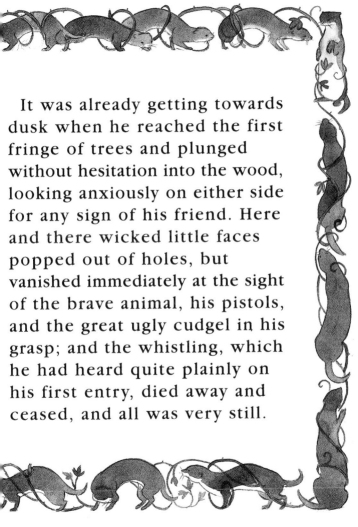

It was already getting towards dusk when he reached the first fringe of trees and plunged without hesitation into the wood, looking anxiously on either side for any sign of his friend. Here and there wicked little faces popped out of holes, but vanished immediately at the sight of the brave animal, his pistols, and the great ugly cudgel in his grasp; and the whistling, which he had heard quite plainly on his first entry, died away and ceased, and all was very still.

The Rat made his way through
the length of the wood to its
furthest edge; then, leaving the
path, he began to explore
every inch of the ground, all
the time calling out cheerfully,
"Moly, Moly, Moly! Where are
you? It's me — it's old Rat!"

He had patiently hunted through the wood for an hour or more, when at last to his joy he heard a little answering cry. Guiding himself by the sound, he made his way through the gathering darkness to the foot of an old beech tree with a hole in it, and from out of the hole came a feeble voice, saying, "Ratty! Is that really you? Oh, I've been so frightened, you can't think!"

The Rat crept into the hollow and there he found the Mole,

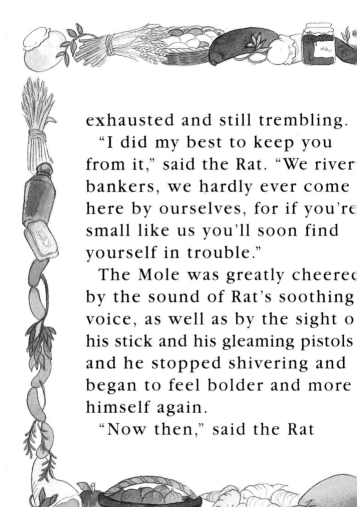

exhausted and still trembling.

"I did my best to keep you from it," said the Rat. "We river bankers, we hardly ever come here by ourselves, for if you're small like us you'll soon find yourself in trouble."

The Mole was greatly cheered by the sound of Rat's soothing voice, as well as by the sight of his stick and his gleaming pistols and he stopped shivering and began to feel bolder and more himself again.

"Now then," said the Rat

presently, "we really must pull ourselves together and make a start for home while there's a still a little light left. It will never do to spend the night here, you understand."

But the poor Mole was too tired to take another step just yet and very soon he was fast asleep amongst the dry leaves. The good-natured Rat lay by his side, patiently waiting, with a pistol in his paw.

When at last the Mole woke up, much refreshed and in his

usual spirits, the Rat put his head out of the hole to check that all was quiet.

"Hullo! hullo! here is a go!" he exclaimed quietly. "It's snowing hard, Mole." The Mole looked out and saw the wood was quite changed. Holes, hollows, pools and pitfalls were all covered by a gleaming carpet of faery snow that looked too delicate to be trodden upon by rough feet. He would not have known it was the same wood and they both silently wondered

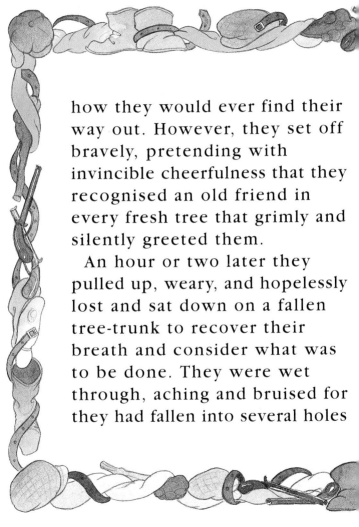

how they would ever find their way out. However, they set off bravely, pretending with invincible cheerfulness that they recognised an old friend in every fresh tree that grimly and silently greeted them.

An hour or two later they pulled up, weary, and hopelessly lost and sat down on a fallen tree-trunk to recover their breath and consider what was to be done. They were wet through, aching and bruised for they had fallen into several holes and now the snow was getting so deep that they could hardly drag their little legs through it. There seemed to be no end to this wood, and no beginning, and worst of all, no way out.

"We must carry on," said the Rat. "The cold is too awful for anything, and the snow will soon be too deep for us to wade through." He peered about him and considered. "Look here," he went on, "there's a sort of dell down there in front of us, where the ground seems all hilly and humpy and hummocky. Let's make our way down there and try and find some sort of cave or hole out of the snow and the wind, and there we'll have a good rest before we try again, for we're both of us dead beat."

So they struggled down into the dell and hunted around one of the hummocky bits, when suddenly the Mole tripped up and fell forward on his face with a squeal.

"Oh, my leg!" he cried. "Oh, my poor shin!" and he sat on

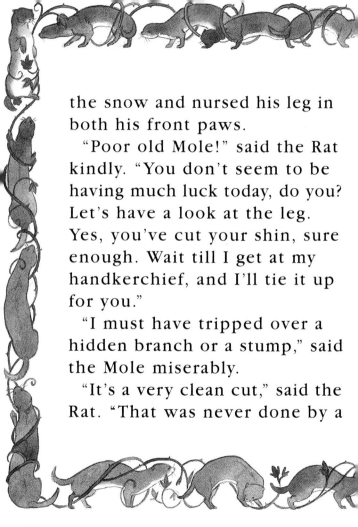

the snow and nursed his leg in both his front paws.

"Poor old Mole!" said the Rat kindly. "You don't seem to be having much luck today, do you? Let's have a look at the leg. Yes, you've cut your shin, sure enough. Wait till I get at my handkerchief, and I'll tie it up for you."

"I must have tripped over a hidden branch or a stump," said the Mole miserably.

"It's a very clean cut," said the Rat. "That was never done by a

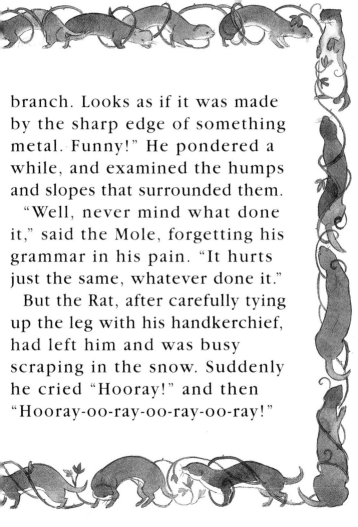

branch. Looks as if it was made by the sharp edge of something metal. Funny!" He pondered a while, and examined the humps and slopes that surrounded them.

"Well, never mind what done it," said the Mole, forgetting his grammar in his pain. "It hurts just the same, whatever done it."

But the Rat, after carefully tying up the leg with his handkerchief, had left him and was busy scraping in the snow. Suddenly he cried "Hooray!" and then "Hooray-oo-ray-oo-ray-oo-ray!"

"Just come and see what I have found, Mole!" cried the delighted Rat. The Mole hobbled to the spot and had a good look.

"Well," he said at last, slowly, "I *see* it right enough. Seen the same sort of thing before, lots of times. A door-scraper! Well, what of it?"

"But don't you see what it *means*, you — you dull-witted animal?" cried the Rat impatiently.

"Of course I see what it means," replied the Mole. "It simply means that some *very* careless and forgetful person has left his door-scraper lying about in the middle of the Wild Wood, *just* where it's *sure* to trip *everybody* up. Very thoughtless of him, I call it!"

"Oh dear! Oh dear!" cried the Rat in despair. "Here, stop arguing and come and scrape!"

After further work his efforts were rewarded, and a very shabby door-mat lay exposed to view.

"There, what did I tell you?" exclaimed the Rat in great triumph.

"Absolutely nothing whatever," replied the Mole, truthfully. "You seem to have found another piece of domestic litter, done for and thrown away, and I suppose you're perfectly happy. Why waste time over such rubbish-heaps, Rat? Can we *eat* a door-mat? Or sleep under a door-mat? Or sit on a door-mat and sledge home over the snow on it, you exasperating rodent!"

"Do — you — mean — to — say," cried the excited Rat, "that this door-mat doesn't *tell* you anything?"

"Really, Rat," said the Mole quite pettishly, "I think we've had enough of this folly. Who ever heard of a door-mat *telling* any one anything? They simply don't do it. Door-mats know their place."

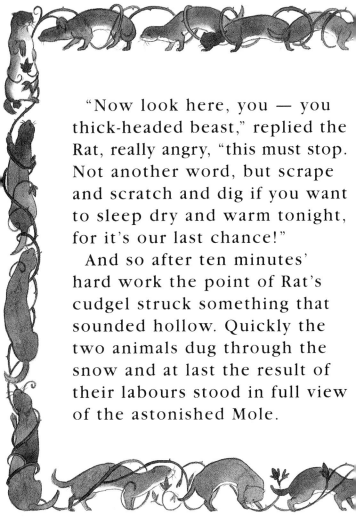

"Now look here, you — you thick-headed beast," replied the Rat, really angry, "this must stop. Not another word, but scrape and scratch and dig if you want to sleep dry and warm tonight, for it's our last chance!"

And so after ten minutes' hard work the point of Rat's cudgel struck something that sounded hollow. Quickly the two animals dug through the snow and at last the result of their labours stood in full view of the astonished Mole.

In the side of what had seemed to be a snow-bank stood a solid-looking little door, painted dark green. An iron bell-pull hung by the side, and below it, on a small brass plate, they could read by the moon light:

MR BADGER

The Mole fell backwards from sheer surprise and delight. "Rat!" he cried humbly, "you are a wonder! A genius! If only I had your wise head, Ratty —"

"But as you haven't," interrupted the Rat rather unkindly, "I suppose you're going to sit on the snow all night and *talk*? Get up at once and hang on to that bell-pull you see there and ring hard while I hammer!"

.While the Rat attacked the door with his stick, the Mole sprang up at the bell-pull and swung there, both feet well off the ground, and from quite a long way off they could faintly hear a deep-toned bell respond.

They waited patiently for what seemed a very long time, stamping in the snow to keep their feet warm. At last they heard the sound of slow shuffling footsteps approaching the door from the inside. There was the noise of a bolt shot back, and the door opened a few inches, enough to show a long snout and a pair of sleepy blinking eyes.

"Now, the *very* next time this happens," said a gruff and suspicious voice, "I shall be exceedingly angry. Who is it

this time, disturbing people on such a night? Speak up!"

"Oh, Badger," cried the Rat, "let us in, please. It's me, Rat, and my friend Mole, and we've lost our way in the snow."

"What, Ratty, my dear little man!" exclaimed the Badger, in quite a different voice. "Come along in, both of you, at once. Why, you must be perished. Well I never! Lost in the snow! And in the Wild Wood too, and at this time of night! But come in with you."

The two animals tumbled over each other in their eagerness to get inside, and heard the door shut behind them with great joy and relief. The Badger wore a long dressing-gown and carpet slippers that were too large for him and very down-at-heel. He carried a flat candlestick in his paw and had probably been on his way to bed when their summons sounded.

"This is not the sort of night for small animals to be out," he said paternally.

"I'm afraid you've been up to some of your pranks again, Ratty. But come along; come into the kitchen. There's a first-rate fire there, and supper and everything."

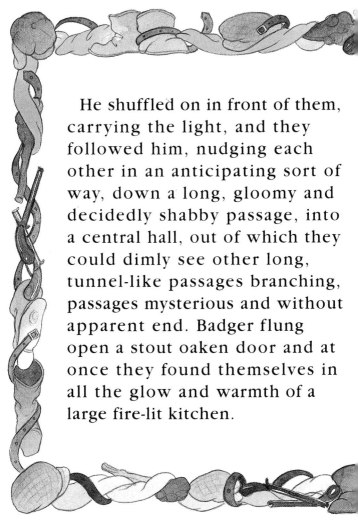

He shuffled on in front of them, carrying the light, and they followed him, nudging each other in an anticipating sort of way, down a long, gloomy and decidedly shabby passage, into a central hall, out of which they could dimly see other long, tunnel-like passages branching, passages mysterious and without apparent end. Badger flung open a stout oaken door and at once they found themselves in all the glow and warmth of a large fire-lit kitchen.

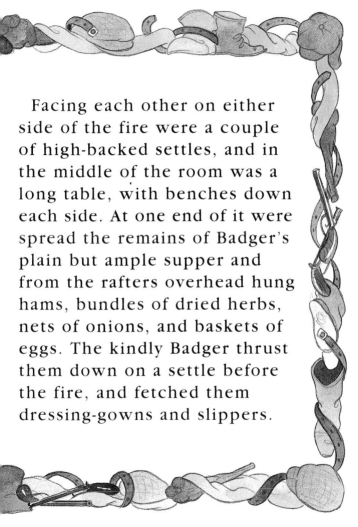

Facing each other on either side of the fire were a couple of high-backed settles, and in the middle of the room was a long table, with benches down each side. At one end of it were spread the remains of Badger's plain but ample supper and from the rafters overhead hung hams, bundles of dried herbs, nets of onions, and baskets of eggs. The kindly Badger thrust them down on a settle before the fire, and fetched them dressing-gowns and slippers.

He bathed and mended Mole's cut till the whole thing was just as good as new, if not better. And so they stretched out in the embracing light and warmth and it seemed as if all that they had suffered was a half-forgotten dream.

Then Badger summoned them
to the table, where he had been
busy laying supper. And so the
hungry animals set to and
conversation was impossible
for a long time. But Badger did

not mind that sort of thing at
all, nor did he take any notice
of elbows on the table, or
everybody speaking at once,
and the Mole began to feel very
friendly towards him.

Supper was finished at last; they gathered round the glowing embers of the great wood fire, and thought how jolly it was to be sitting up *so* late, and *so* full. Then the Badger said heartily, "Now! tell us news from your part of the world. How's old Toad going on?"

Their good friend, the Toad, had lately shown much interest in motor-cars. Indeed a passion for these things had quite overtaken him and he had lost interest in all other things save driving at speed in a shiny metal vehicle along the narrow country lanes. Consequently, he suffered many crashes and, as the Rat told the Badger, his coach-house was now piled up to the roof with fragments of motor-cars, none of them bigger than Badger's night-cap!

"He's been in hospital three times," put in the Mole, "and as for the fines he's had to pay, it's simply awful to think of."

"That's part of the trouble," continued the Rat. "Toad's

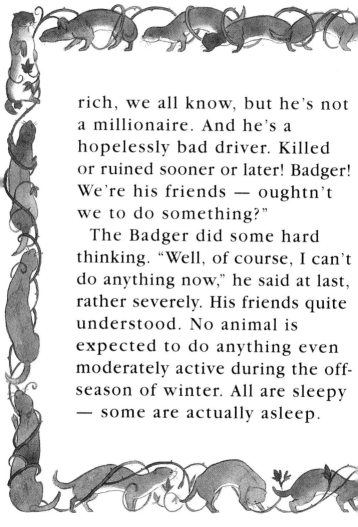

rich, we all know, but he's not a millionaire. And he's a hopelessly bad driver. Killed or ruined sooner or later! Badger! We're his friends — oughtn't we to do something?"

The Badger did some hard thinking. "Well, of course, I can't do anything now," he said at last, rather severely. His friends quite understood. No animal is expected to do anything even moderately active during the off-season of winter. All are sleepy — some are actually asleep.

"But when the year has really turned, and the nights are shorter, well, then we'll take Toad seriously in hand. We'll stand no nonsense whatever. We'll make him be a sensible Toad. We'll — you're asleep, Rat!"

"Not me!" said the Rat, waking up with a jerk.

"Come along, it's time we were all in bed," said the Badger, with a smile. "I'll show you your quarters — and take your time tomorrow morning — breakfast at any hour you please!"

And so they were led to a long
room half-filled with Badger's
winter stores, piles of apples,
turnips and potatoes, baskets
full of nuts, and jars of honey;
but the two little white beds
looked soft and inviting and
the Mole and the Water Rat
tumbled in between the sheets
in great joy and contentment.

The next morning the two tired animals came down to breakfast very late and found a bright fire burning in the kitchen, and two young hedgehogs sitting on a bench at the table, eating porridge out of wooden bowls.

"We set off for school early this morning," explained one of them, earnestly, "but we lost our way in the snow and just happened to come across Mr Badger's door and knowing what a kind gentleman he is, we knocked and, well, he just happened to have a big pot of porridge on the go."

"I understand perfectly," said the Rat, with a twinkle in his eye. "And where is Mr Badger?"

"The master's gone to his study and said he is busy and on no account is he to be disturbed." The Rat understood this perfectly, too. Badger would be snoozing with his feet up on the desk and a red spotted handkerchief over his face, being "busy" in his usual way at this time of the year.

The front-door bell clanged loudly and Billy, the smaller hedgehog, scurried off to see who it might be. Soon he arrived with the Otter, who threw himself on the Rat with an embrace and a shout of joy.

"Thought I should find you here all right," he said cheerfully. "They were all in a great state of alarm along River Bank when I arrived this morning. Rat never been home all night — nor Mole either — something dreadful must have happened, they said.

"But I knew that when people were in any fix they mostly went to Badger, so I came straight here, through the Wild Wood, in all the snow!"

The Mole shivered at the thought and some of yesterday's terror came back to him at the mention of the Wild Wood.

Then in came the Badger, yawning and rubbing his eyes and greeting them all in his quiet, simple way, with kind inquiries for every one. "It must be getting on for lunch time," he remarked.

The two hedgehogs looked up
eagerly but were too shy to say
anything and with a sixpence
apiece and a pat on the head
from Mr Badger, they went off
with much respectful swinging
of caps and touching of forelocks.

Presently they all sat down to lunch together and the Mole lost no time in telling Mr Badger how comfortable and homely he found his hole to be.

"Once well underground," replied the Badger, "you know exactly where you are. Nothing can happen to you, and nothing can get at you. No tradesmen, no *weather*. Things go on overhead, and you let 'em and don't bother about 'em. When you want to, up you go, and there the things are, waiting for you."

The Mole simply beamed at him. That was exactly how he felt about his own home. Rat's house and Toad's great hall were all very well but underground was the place to be, without a doubt! And to the Mole's great delight, straight after lunch, while the other two were arguing about eels, the Badger lighted a lantern and took him on a tour. Mole was staggered at the size, the extent of it all. The length of the dim passages, the pillars, the arches, the vaulted ceilings.

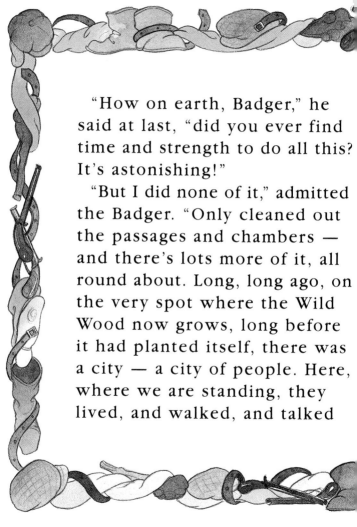

"How on earth, Badger," he said at last, "did you ever find time and strength to do all this? It's astonishing!"

"But I did none of it," admitted the Badger. "Only cleaned out the passages and chambers — and there's lots more of it, all round about. Long, long ago, on the very spot where the Wild Wood now grows, long before it had planted itself, there was a city — a city of people. Here, where we are standing, they lived, and walked, and talked

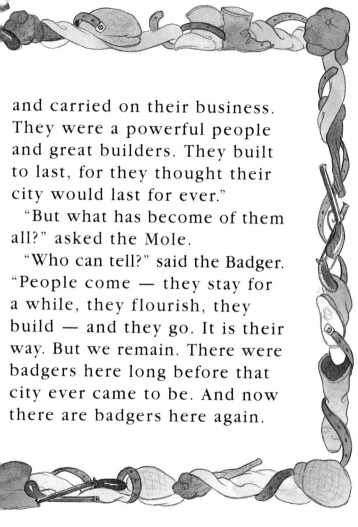

and carried on their business.
They were a powerful people
and great builders. They built
to last, for they thought their
city would last for ever."

"But what has become of them
all?" asked the Mole.

"Who can tell?" said the Badger.
"People come — they stay for
a while, they flourish, they
build — and they go. It is their
way. But we remain. There were
badgers here long before that
city ever came to be. And now
there are badgers here again.

"We are an enduring lot. After the people went, the wind and rain took the matter in hand and over the years the buildings fell down and the seeds and trees grew up and bramble and fern came creeping in to help. Sand and soil clogged and covered and in course of time our home was ready for us again, and we moved in. And up above us other animals arrived and settled down. The Wild Wood is pretty well populated by now, with all the usual lot, good, bad and indifferent — I name no names," he said quietly, and the Mole shivered.

The Badger patted him kindly on the shoulder. "They're not so bad really, and we must all live and let live. But I'll pass the word round tomorrow, and I think you'll have no further trouble."

When they got back to the kitchen the Water Rat was pacing up and down restlessly. He found the underground atmosphere oppressive and longed to get back to the River Bank.

"Come along, Mole," he said anxiously. "We must be off while it's daylight."

"You really needn't fret, Ratty," said the Badger. "My passages run further than you think, and reach to the edge of the wood in several directions. You can leave by one of my short cuts." And so the Badger led the way along a damp and airless tunnel for a long and weary distance. At last daylight began to show itself through tangled growth over-hanging the entrance.

There the Badger bidded
them a hasty goodbye and
pushed them hurriedly through
the opening. Then he rearranged
the creepers to make
everything look as natural as
possible again, and retreated.

They found themselves standing
on the very edge of the Wild
Wood and ahead of them,
beyond a great space of quiet
fields, was a glint of the familiar
old river. The Otter led them on
a bee-line for a distant stile and
from there they looked back
and saw the whole mass of the
Wild Wood, dense and menacing.

Together they turned away and after a while the Rat and the Otter said farewell and headed for the river. And as the Mole hurried along, he saw clearly that he was an animal of tilled field and hedgerow. For others, the hard and stubborn endurance that went with Nature in the rough; he must be wise, must keep to the pleasant places in which his lines were laid and which held adventure enough, in their way, to last a lifetime.

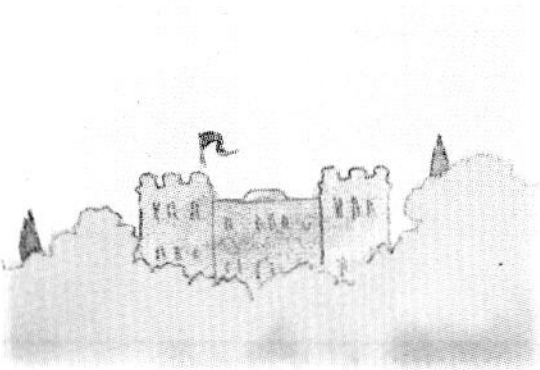

CHAPTER 3
Return to
Toad Hall

The Rat was just wondering what to do one fine sunny morning when he heard a strange gurgling sound coming from right outside his door. Imagine his surprise when he found that it was none other than Mr Toad, struggling to keep afloat in the rippling, rolling waters of the river, and dressed in a most curious dress and bonnet! Now Toad had been missing for quite some time. The Mole and the Water Rat had heard some terrible tales of what had befallen him — that he had stolen a motor car, been thrown in gaol, and all sorts of other dreadful things. Rat was not at all surprised at the sight of his old friend in yet another curious situation. So he gripped the spluttering Toad firmly by the scruff of the neck, and pulled him over the edge of the hole.

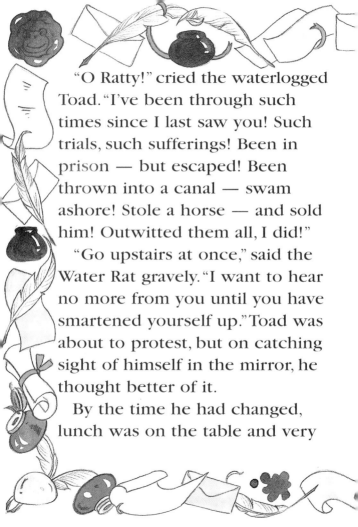

"O Ratty!" cried the waterlogged Toad. "I've been through such times since I last saw you! Such trials, such sufferings! Been in prison — but escaped! Been thrown into a canal — swam ashore! Stole a horse — and sold him! Outwitted them all, I did!"

"Go upstairs at once," said the Water Rat gravely. "I want to hear no more from you until you have smartened yourself up." Toad was about to protest, but on catching sight of himself in the mirror, he thought better of it.

By the time he had changed, lunch was on the table and very

glad Toad was to see it. While they ate, Toad recounted his adventures but the more he talked, the more grave the Water Rat became.

"Now Toad," said the Rat, when the Toad paused for breath. "I don't want to hurt your feelings, but don't you see what an awful ass you're making of yourself. You have been imprisoned, starved, chased, jeered at and flung into the water, and all because of a motor car! Whenever are you going to start being sensible, and think of your friends?"

Toad looked at the Rat with a wounded expression as he continued. "Do you suppose it's any pleasure to me, for instance, to hear animals saying, as I go about, that I'm the chap that keeps company with gaol-birds!"

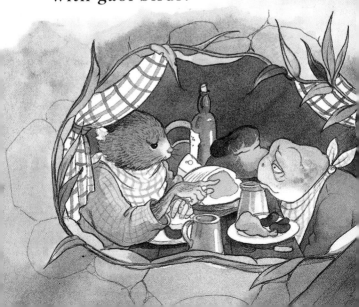

Now, it was a very comforting point in Toad's character that he was a thoroughly good-hearted animal, and never minded being ticked off by those who were his real friends. And even when most set upon a thing, he was always able to see the other side of the question. So although, while the Rat was talking so seriously, he kept saying to himself mutinously, "But it *was* fun, though! Great fun!" and making strange secret noises inside him, k-i-ck-ck-ck, and poop-p-p, and such-like, yet when the Rat had quite finished, he heaved a deep sigh. "You are quite right, Ratty," he said humbly. "Yes, I've been a conceited old ass, I can quite see that, but now I'm going to be a good Toad, and not do it any more. As for motor-cars, I've not been at all so keen about them since my last ducking in that river of yours. The fact is, while I was hanging on to the edge of your hole and getting my breath back, I had a sudden brilliant idea connected with motor-boats —

there, there! don't take on so, old chap, and stamp; it was only an idea, and we won't talk any more about it now. We'll have our coffee and then I'm going to stroll gently down to Toad Hall and get into clothes of my own and forget all about adventures. I shall lead a quiet, respectable life and give up the idea of motor-cars all together."

"Stroll down to Toad Hall?" cried the Rat, greatly excited. "What are you talking about? Do you mean to say you haven't heard?"

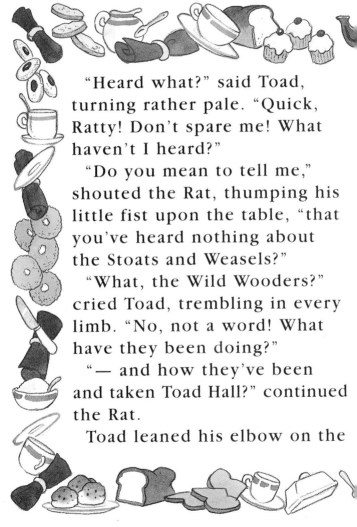

"Heard what?" said Toad, turning rather pale. "Quick, Ratty! Don't spare me! What haven't I heard?"

"Do you mean to tell me," shouted the Rat, thumping his little fist upon the table, "that you've heard nothing about the Stoats and Weasels?"

"What, the Wild Wooders?" cried Toad, trembling in every limb. "No, not a word! What have they been doing?"

"— and how they've been and taken Toad Hall?" continued the Rat.

Toad leaned his elbow on the

table, and his chin on his hands; and tears welled up in his eyes and splashed on the table. "Tell me all, Ratty," he wept. So the Rat told him the whole sorry tale.

"When the Wild Wood animals heard what had happened to you — I mean, when you — disappeared from society for a time —" Toad merely nodded. "Well, they said hard things and served you right. They got very cocky, and went about saying you would never come back again, never, never!" Toad nodded silently.

"Well, Mole and Badger, they stuck up for you and moved their things into Toad Hall and looked after it for you so that it would be ready for you when you turned up," said the Rat.

"But one dark night," he continued, "when it was raining cats and dogs, a band of weasels, armed to the teeth, crept silently up the drive to the front door. At the same time a body of desperate

ferrets stole through the kitchen-garden, while a company of skirmishing stoats took over the conservatory and the billiard-room, and held the French windows opening on to the lawn."

"Then later, as the Mole and the Badger were sitting quietly by the fire in the drawing-room, all unsuspecting, those bloodthirsty villains broke down the doors and rushed in upon them from every side.

"But what could they do? They were unarmed and surrounded. Then those beastly animals took them and turned them out into the cold and the wet, with many insulting and uncalled-for remarks!"

Here the unfeeling Toad broke into a snigger, then quickly pulled himself together and tried to look solemn.

"And the Wild Wooders have been living in Toad Hall ever since," continued the Rat. "They lie in bed half the day and the place is in such a mess! They eat your grub and make bad jokes about you, and sing vulgar songs — about prisons and policemen — and they're telling everyone that they've come to stay for good."

"O, have they!" said Toad, getting up and seizing a stick. "I'll jolly soon see about that!"

"It's no good, Toad!" called the Rat despairingly, but the Toad was gone, marching rapidly down the road. But as he approached his own front gate a long mean-looking ferret with a gun popped up from behind the palings.

"Who goes there?" said the ferret sharply.

"Stuff and nonsense!" said Toad very angrily. With that the ferret raised his gun and a bullet whistled over Toad's head. Hastily he scrambled to his feet and scampered off down the road as hard as he could, while the ferret laughed cruelly behind him.

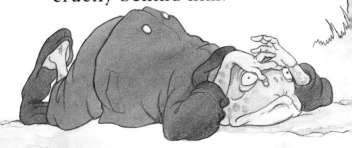

"What did I tell you?" said the Rat when he returned. "They have armed sentries posted everywhere." But the Toad was determined not to give in. He got out the Rat's boat and rowed up the river until he reached Toad Hall. All seemed quiet and still, but just as he paddled warily under the bridge . . . *Crash!* Two gleeful stoats dropped a huge stone from overhead and it smashed straight through the bottom of the boat. "Your turn next, Toady!" they cried as the indignant Toad swam to shore.

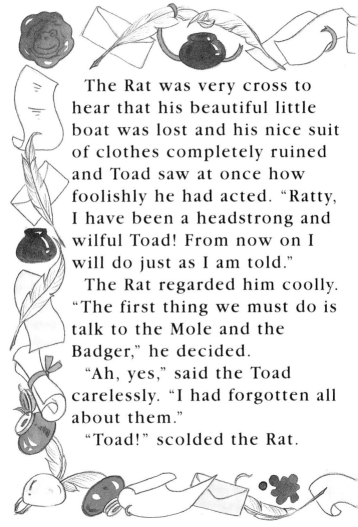

The Rat was very cross to hear that his beautiful little boat was lost and his nice suit of clothes completely ruined and Toad saw at once how foolishly he had acted. "Ratty, I have been a headstrong and wilful Toad! From now on I will do just as I am told."

The Rat regarded him coolly. "The first thing we must do is talk to the Mole and the Badger," he decided.

"Ah, yes," said the Toad carelessly. "I had forgotten all about them."

"Toad!" scolded the Rat.

"While you were riding about the country in expensive motor-cars and galloping proudly on horses, those poor devoted animals have been camping out in the open, in very rough conditions, keeping watch over your house. You don't deserve to have such true and loyal friends, Toad, and some day you'll be sorry you didn't appreciate them more!" Then Toad shed bitter tears. "I'm an ungrateful beast," he sobbed. "Let me go out now into the dark, cold night and find them, and share their hardships, and — hold on a bit! Surely I heard the chink of dishes on a tray. Supper's here at last, hooray!"

The Rat sighed heavily but reminded himself that poor Toad had been on prison fare for a long time and had a lot of catching up to do.

They had just finished their meal when a heavy knock was heard upon the door. It was Mr Badger and the Mole. They looked very shabby and tousled but the Mole beamed broadly when he caught sight of Toad.

"Hooray! Here's old Toad!"
he cried. "Why, you must have
managed to escape, you clever,
intelligent Toad!"

Toad's chest puffed up
alarmingly. "Oh, no," he said.
"Not *really* clever. Only
broken out of the strongest
prison in England, captured a
railway train and stolen a
horse, that's all!" "My, my!"
said the Mole admiringly. "You
must tell me all about it!" Toad
beamed but the Rat frowned
disapprovingly. "Stop egging
him on, Mole," he said. "Tell us
what is happening at Toad Hall

and what's best to be done."

"The position's about as bad as it can be," replied the Mole grumpily. "Sentries and guns everywhere."

"Quite useless to think of attacking the place," added the Badger. "They're too strong for us." The Toad clutched a sofa cushion and sobbed into it. "Then it's all over," he wept.

"Cheer up, Toady!" said the Badger. "There are more ways of getting back a place than taking it by storm. I have a secret!" Toad sat up slowly and dried his eyes.

"There — is — an — underground — passage," said the Badger impressively, "that leads from the river bank right up into the middle of Toad Hall." Toad's eyes grew as round as saucers. "There is going to be a big banquet tomorrow night," went on the Badger. "It's the Chief Weasel's birthday, and all the weasels will be celebrating; eating, drinking, suspecting nothing! No guns, no swords, no sticks! And the tunnel leads right up under the butler's pantry, next to the dining-hall!"

"We shall creep out very quietly —" cried the Mole.

"— with our pistols and sticks —" shouted the Rat.

"— and rush in upon them," said the Badger.

"— and whack 'em, and whack 'em, and whack 'em!" cried the Toad joyfully.

They all agreed that this was
a splendid plan and so went to
bed happy and content.

When Toad came down next
morning he found the Rat
sorting their weapons into
neat little piles and the Badger
calmly reading his newspaper.

Soon the Mole came tumbling into the room, very pleased with himself. "I've been having such fun teasing the stoats!" he said. "I put on Toad's old washerwoman dress and off I went to Toad Hall. The sergeant on charge told me to run away, but I said 'Run away? It won't be *me* that'll be running away in a very short time from now! A hundred bloodthirsty badgers, six boatloads of rats, and a picked body of the Death-or-Glory Toads, will be storming Toad Hall this very night!'

"Ho, ho! You should have seen their faces. 'There won't be much left of you by the time they've finished, unless you clear out while you still have the chance!' I said, then I ran off quickly!"

"O, *Moly*, how could you?" said the Rat, dismayed.

"You've spoilt everything!" cried Toad, but the Badger spoke quietly. "Mole," he said. "I see you have more sense in your little finger than some other animals have in the whole of their fat bodies. Good Mole! Clever Mole!"

The Toad was simply wild with jealousy, especially as he couldn't make out for the life of him what the Mole had done that was so particularly clever.

When it began to grow dark, they all armed themselves and made ready. Then the Badger took a dark lantern in one paw, grasped his great stick with the other, and said, "Now then, follow me!" He led them along by the river for a little way, and then suddenly swung himself over the edge and into a hole in the river bank.

The Mole, the Rat and Toad
followed him. Now they were
in the secret passage and the
expedition had really begun! It
was cold, and dark, and damp,
and low, and narrow.

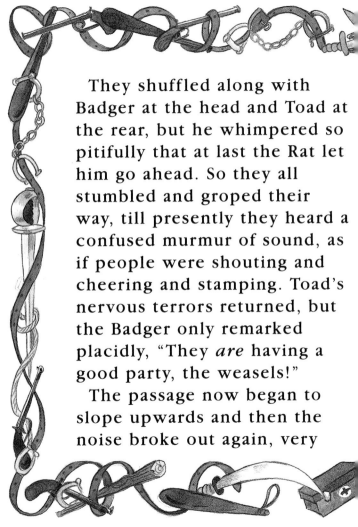

They shuffled along with Badger at the head and Toad at the rear, but he whimpered so pitifully that at last the Rat let him go ahead. So they all stumbled and groped their way, till presently they heard a confused murmur of sound, as if people were shouting and cheering and stamping. Toad's nervous terrors returned, but the Badger only remarked placidly, "They *are* having a good party, the weasels!"

The passage now began to slope upwards and then the noise broke out again, very

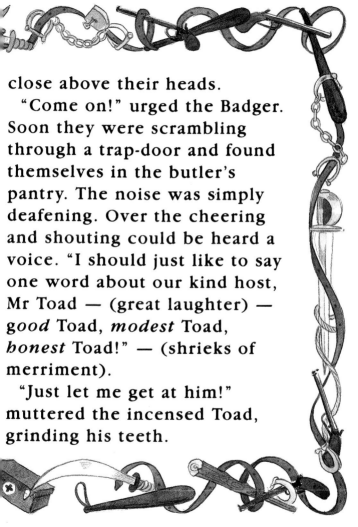

close above their heads.

"Come on!" urged the Badger. Soon they were scrambling through a trap-door and found themselves in the butler's pantry. The noise was simply deafening. Over the cheering and shouting could be heard a voice. "I should just like to say one word about our kind host, Mr Toad — (great laughter) — *good* Toad, *modest* Toad, *honest* Toad!" — (shrieks of merriment).

"Just let me get at him!" muttered the incensed Toad, grinding his teeth.

"Let me sing you a little song," went on the voice, "on the subject of Toad!"

The Badger drew himself up, got a good firm grip of his stick with both paws, and cried: "The hour is come, my friends! Follow me!"

He flung the door open wide.
My! What a squealing and a
squeaking and a screeching
filled the air! Terrified weasels
dived under the tables and
sprang madly up at the
windows!

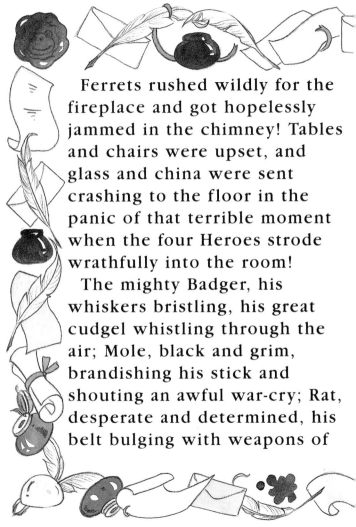

Ferrets rushed wildly for the fireplace and got hopelessly jammed in the chimney! Tables and chairs were upset, and glass and china were sent crashing to the floor in the panic of that terrible moment when the four Heroes strode wrathfully into the room!

The mighty Badger, his whiskers bristling, his great cudgel whistling through the air; Mole, black and grim, brandishing his stick and shouting an awful war-cry; Rat, desperate and determined, his belt bulging with weapons of

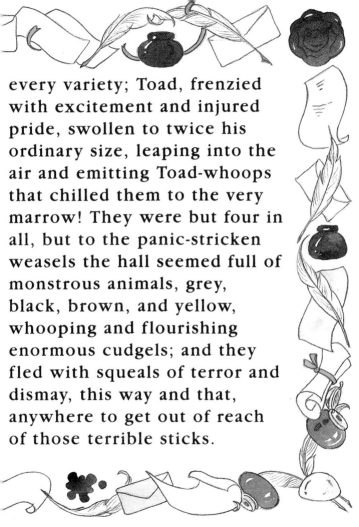

every variety; Toad, frenzied
with excitement and injured
pride, swollen to twice his
ordinary size, leaping into the
air and emitting Toad-whoops
that chilled them to the very
marrow! They were but four in
all, but to the panic-stricken
weasels the hall seemed full of
monstrous animals, grey,
black, brown, and yellow,
whooping and flourishing
enormous cudgels; and they
fled with squeals of terror and
dismay, this way and that,
anywhere to get out of reach
of those terrible sticks.

The affair was soon over. Up
and down strode the four
Friends, whacking with their
sticks, and in five minutes the
room was cleared. The Badger
leant on his stick and wiped
his honest brow.

"Mole," he said, "you're the best of fellows! Just nip outside and make sure there are no stoat-sentries lurking about. I've an idea that, thanks to you, we shan't have much trouble from *them* tonight!"

Then the hungry animals' thoughts turned to supper. "Stir your stumps, Toad, and look lively!" urged the Badger. Toad bustled about finding food and they were just sitting down to a fine meal when the Mole clambered in through the window, chuckling to himself.

"It's all over," he reported.

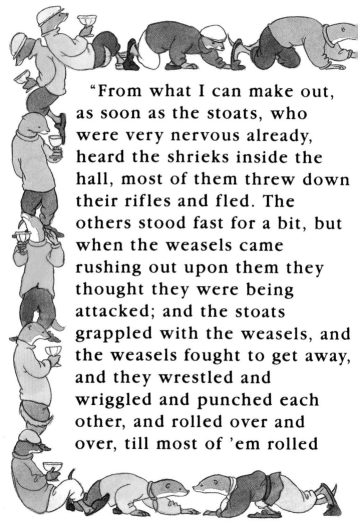

"From what I can make out, as soon as the stoats, who were very nervous already, heard the shrieks inside the hall, most of them threw down their rifles and fled. The others stood fast for a bit, but when the weasels came rushing out upon them they thought they were being attacked; and the stoats grappled with the weasels, and the weasels fought to get away, and they wrestled and wriggled and punched each other, and rolled over and over, till most of 'em rolled

into the river!"

"Excellent animal!" said the Badger, his mouth full of chicken and trifle. Then Mole pulled his chair up to the table and pitched in, and Toad, like the gentleman he was, put all his jealousy from him, and said heartily, "Thank you kindly, dear Mole, for all your trouble tonight, and especially for your cleverness this morning!" The Badger was pleased at that, and said, "There spoke my brave Toad!" So they finished their supper in great joy and contentment.

Presently they made their way upstairs and were soon tucked up in clean beds, safe in Toad's ancestral home, won back by great bravery, cunning planning, and a proper handling of sticks.

The following morning, Toad, who had overslept as usual, came down to breakfast disgracefully late. Through the French windows he could see the Mole and the Water Rat sitting in wicker chairs out on the lawn, telling each other stories and roaring with laughter. Badger was deep in the morning paper and he merely nodded as Toad entered the room. Badger let him finish his breakfast, then looked up and spoke. "There's a lot of work to be done," he said gravely.

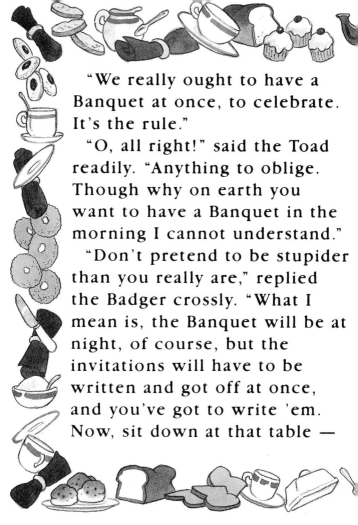

"We really ought to have a Banquet at once, to celebrate. It's the rule."

"O, all right!" said the Toad readily. "Anything to oblige. Though why on earth you want to have a Banquet in the morning I cannot understand."

"Don't pretend to be stupider than you really are," replied the Badger crossly. "What I mean is, the Banquet will be at night, of course, but the invitations will have to be written and got off at once, and you've got to write 'em. Now, sit down at that table —

there's stacks of letter-paper on it, with 'Toad Hall' at the top in blue and gold — and write invitations to all our friends. I'll order the food."

"What!" cried Toad, dismayed. "Me stop indoors and write a lot of rotten letters on a jolly morning like this when I want to swagger around my property and enjoy myself! Certainly not! I'll be — I'll see you – stop a minute, though! Why, of course, dear Badger! What is my pleasure compared with that of others!" Badger looked at him warily.

"You wish it done, and it shall be done," continued Toad. "Go, Badger, order what food you like, then join our young friends outside in their innocent mirth, oblivious of me and my cares." The Badger's suspicions deepened, but Toad's honest face beamed back at him.

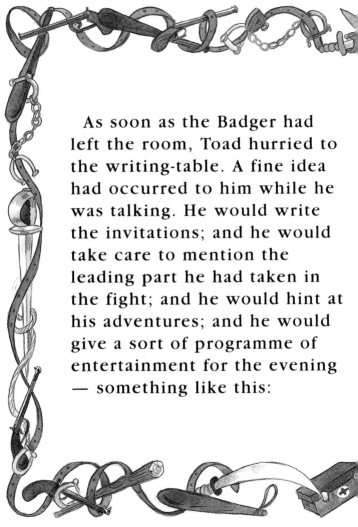

As soon as the Badger had left the room, Toad hurried to the writing-table. A fine idea had occurred to him while he was talking. He would write the invitations; and he would take care to mention the leading part he had taken in the fight; and he would hint at his adventures; and he would give a sort of programme of entertainment for the evening — something like this:

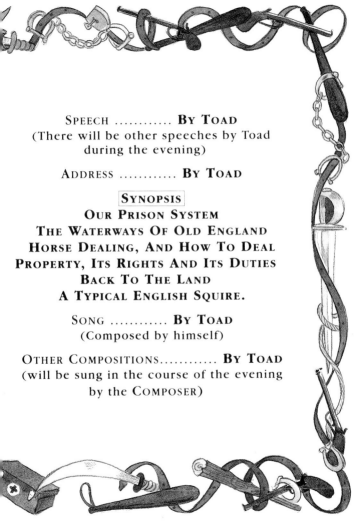

SPEECH .... **BY TOAD**
(There will be other speeches by Toad
during the evening)

ADDRESS .... **BY TOAD**

SYNOPSIS
OUR PRISON SYSTEM
THE WATERWAYS OF OLD ENGLAND
HORSE DEALING, AND HOW TO DEAL
PROPERTY, ITS RIGHTS AND ITS DUTIES
BACK TO THE LAND
A TYPICAL ENGLISH SQUIRE.

SONG .... **BY TOAD**
(Composed by himself)

OTHER COMPOSITIONS............ **BY TOAD**
(will be sung in the course of the evening
by the COMPOSER)

The idea pleased him mightily, and Toad worked very hard and got all the letters finished by noon. A small and rather bedraggled weasel volunteered his services and was quickly sent off to post them.

When the other animals returned for lunch, they looked doubtfully at Toad, expecting to find him sulky and depressed. Instead he was so uppish and inflated that they began to suspect something. How well they knew their friend, Toad!

"Now, look here, Toad," said the Rat. "We want you to understand clearly, once and for all, that there are going to be no speeches and no songs at this Banquet. We're not arguing with you; we're just telling you."

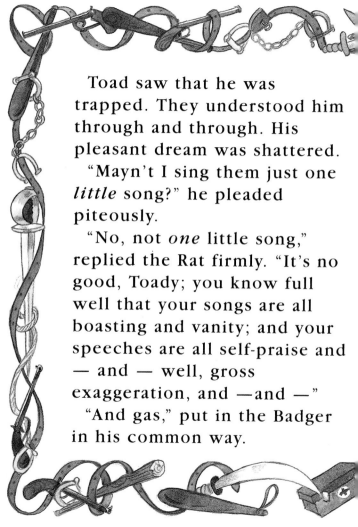

Toad saw that he was trapped. They understood him through and through. His pleasant dream was shattered.

"Mayn't I sing them just one *little* song?" he pleaded piteously.

"No, not *one* little song," replied the Rat firmly. "It's no good, Toady; you know full well that your songs are all boasting and vanity; and your speeches are all self-praise and — and — well, gross exaggeration, and —and —"

"And gas," put in the Badger in his common way.

"You *must* turn over a new leaf," went on the Rat, "and now seems a splendid time to begin."

Toad remained a long while plunged in thought. At last he raised his head. "You have won, my friends," he said, brokenly. "It was just a small thing to ask — merely permission to let myself go and hear the applause that always seems to me — somehow — to bring out my best qualities. However, you are right, I know, and I am wrong." He hung his head.

"Henceforth I will be a very different Toad. But, O dear, O dear, this is a hard world!" And pressing his handkerchief to his face, he left the room with faltering footsteps.

"Badger," said the Rat. "I feel like a brute."

"I know, I know," said the Badger gloomily. "But Toad has to live here and be respected. Would you have him a common laughing-stock, mocked and jeered by stoats and weasels?"

"Of course not," said the Rat. "And, talking of weasels, it's lucky we came upon that little weasel, just as he was setting out with Toad's invitations. They were simply disgraceful and I confiscated the lot. The Mole is filling up plain, simple invitation cards right now."

At last the hour for the banquet began to draw near and Toad was still sitting in his bedroom, melancholy and thoughtful. He pondered long and deeply. Gradually his frown cleared, and he began to smile long, slow smiles. Then he took to giggling, and at last he got up, locked the door, drew the curtains, collected all the chairs in the room and arranged them in a semi-circle, and took up his position in front of them, swelling visibly. Then he bowed, coughed twice, and began to sing.

TOAD'S LAST LITTLE SONG!

The Toad — came — home!
There was panic in the parlour
and howling in the hall,
There was crying in the cow-shed
and shrieking in the stall,
When the Toad — came —home!

When the Toad — came —home!
There was smashing in of window
and crashing in of door,
There was chivvying of weasels
that fainted on the floor,
When the Toad — came — home!

Bang! go the drums!
The trumpeters are tooting
and the soldiers are saluting,
And the cannon
they are shooting and
the motor-cars are hooting,
As the — Hero — comes!

Shout — Hoo-ray!
And let each one of the crowd try
and shout it very loud,
In honour of an animal
of whom you're justly proud,
For it's Toad's — great — day!

He sang this very loud, with great expression; and when he had done, he sang it all over again. Then he heaved a deep sigh, a long sigh, and went down to greet his guests.

All the animals cheered when he entered, and crowded round to congratulate him and praise his courage, but Toad only smiled faintly and murmured "Not at all! On the contrary! Badger was the mastermind, the Mole and the Water Rat bore the brunt of the fighting, I merely served in the ranks and did little or nothing."

The animals were greatly puzzled by this unexpected attitude of his; and Toad felt, as he moved from one guest to the other, making his modest responses, that he was an object of absorbing interest to every one.

The Badger had ordered the best of everything and the banquet was a great success. There was much talking and laughter, but through it all Toad merely murmured pleasant nothings to the animals on either side of him. From time to time he stole a

glance at the Badger and the Rat, and always when he looked they were staring at each other with their mouths open; and this gave him the greatest satisfaction. There were some knockings on the table from some of the livelier and younger animals, and cries of "Speech! Song! Mr Toad!" But Toad only shook his head gently, raised one paw in mild protest and managed to convey to them that this dinner was being run on strictly conventional lines. He was indeed an altered Toad!

After this celebration, the four animals continued to lead their lives in great joy and contentment, undisturbed by further risings or invasions.

Toad, after due consultation with his friends, selected a handsome gold chain and locket set with pearls, which he sent to the gaoler's daughter with a letter that even the Badger admitted was modest, grateful, and appreciative; and the engine-driver, in his turn, was properly thanked and compensated for all his pains and trouble. Even the barge-woman was found and paid the full value of her horse, something which Toad grumbled over a great deal.

Sometimes, in the course of long summer evenings, the friends would take a stroll together in the Wild Wood, now successfully tamed so far as they were concerned.

It was pleasing to see how respectfully they were greeted by the inhabitants, and how the mother-weasels would bring their young ones to the mouths of their holes, and say, pointing, "Look, baby! There goes the great Mr Toad! And that's the gallant Water Rat, a terrible fighter, walking along with him. And here comes the famous Mr Mole, of whom you so often have heard your father tell!" But when their infants were naughty and quite beyond control, they would quiet them by telling how, if they didn't hush, the terrible grey Badger would up and get them. This was, in point of fact, most unfair and misleading, for Badger, although he cared little about Society, was rather fond of children; but it never failed to have its full effect.